AMAZING AMBER

AND HER LAZY LASER EYE

Written and created by
Eagle Ngo, Mitchell Bagley and Jason Cheng
Illustrated by
Aleksic Vladimir

Published by Cheng Ophthalmology Pty Ltd 2018

Unit 18, Jindalee Allsports Shopping Village

19 Kooringal Drive

Jindalee QLD 4074

Australia

info@amazingamberbooks.com

A catalogue record for this book is available from the National Library of Australia.

Book cover design and formatting services by BookCoverCafe.com

First edition 2018

ISBN 978-0-6483744-2-8 (pbk)
ISBN 978-0-6483744-1-1 (ebk)

Foreword

Young children with amblyopia, sometimes referred to as 'lazy vision', are in a tricky situation. They may be at an age where the weaker eye can be made to see better by using it, but are too young to understand beyond their dislike of wearing an eye patch. By the time they are old enough to understand and cooperate, it may be too late to get the brain to use the amblyopic eye. They need all the assistance they can find to help them feel good about wearing an eye patch and making the weak eye stronger, including the assistance of superhero Amazing Amber.

This story aims to help children identify positively with Amber, and become superheroes themselves. Amblyopia treatment does require a heroic effort on the part of carers and children. Read this book over and over to your child to reinforce the good they are doing when patching their eye.

Dr Stephen Hing
Past Head of Ophthalmology at The Children's Hospital at Westmead, Sydney

Amazing Amber is a superhero.

She loves to play with her friends in the park.

She loves to fly high above the clouds.

But most of all, she loves to help people.

Pie-throwing Pete is a mean bully.

He likes to
make pies.

He likes to
eat pies.

But most of all, he likes to *throw* pies.

No one likes it when Pie-throwing Pete throws pies, especially when he throws his pies at them.

Amazing Amber always saves the day by shooting down the pies with her laser eyes.

One day Pie-throwing Pete has an idea. He builds a new machine that throws two pies at the same time.

The next time Pie-throwing Pete throws his pies, Amazing Amber comes to save the day like she always does.

She shoots down one pie with one of her laser eyes, but ...

SPLAT!

Instead, she gets a pie in her eye.

'Ha-ha! I got you!' laughs Pie-throwing Pete.

Amazing Amber is confused. She doesn't know why one of her eyes is weaker than the other.

Amazing Amber goes to the eye doctor, Dr Teddy.

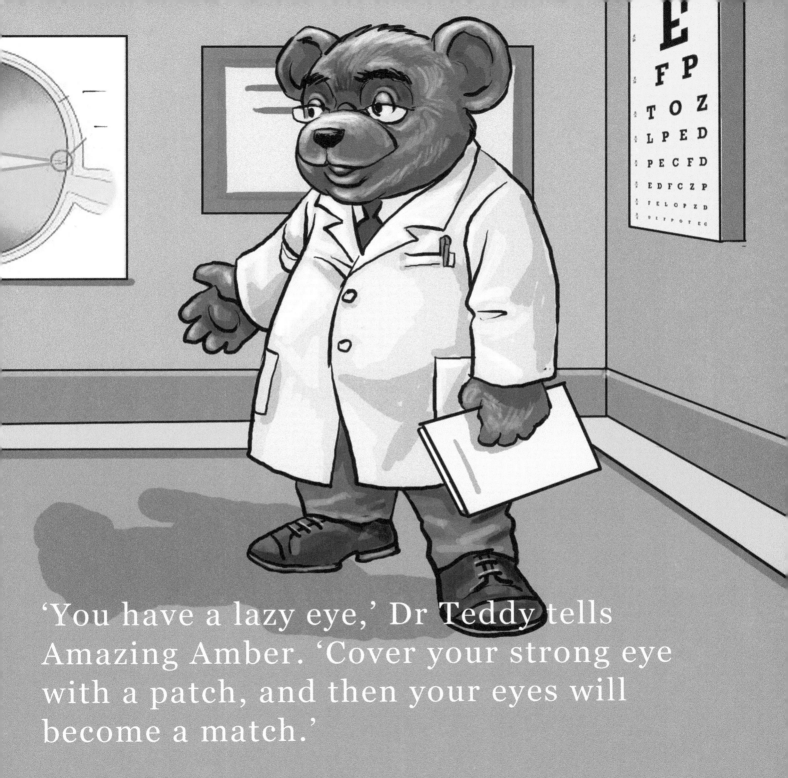

'You have a lazy eye,' Dr Teddy tells Amazing Amber. 'Cover your strong eye with a patch, and then your eyes will become a match.'

Amazing Amber wears her eye patch on her strong eye every day.

Her weak eye becomes stronger ...

... and stronger ...

... and stronger!

Finally Doctor Teddy tells her that both her eyes are strong. 'Your eyes are a match, and you no longer need to wear your patch.'

Amazing Amber takes off her patch. 'Hooray!' she says. Now both her laser eyes are strong.

The next day, Pie-throwing Pete starts throwing pies again.

'Are you ready to get another pie in the eye?' he asks Amazing Amber.

'Not this time, Pie-throwing Pete,' Amazing Amber says. 'I've been wearing my patch, so now *both* my laser eyes are strong.'

Pie-throwing Pete doesn't believe Amazing Amber. He throws two pies at her.

Amazing Amber shoots down both pies with her laser eyes.

Then she destroys the pie-throwing machine.

'Oh, no!' Pie-throwing Pete yells, and runs away.

Everyone cheers, 'Hooray!' Thanks to her patch, Amazing Amber has saved the day once again.

Stick your patch onto one of Amazing Amber's laser eyes.

About the Authors

Eagle Ngo is a year-12 student from Brisbane who, after learning about the works of Dr Fred Hollows, was inspired to contribute to his cause. Eagle began fundraising for the Fred Hollows Foundation at the age of eleven by selling food and raffle tickets at a local fair and Rotary club. In addition, he has also raised $5000 making and selling clay figures through his own website. Eagle hopes that this book will make eye patches and doctors a little less scary for children with amblyopia (commonly known as lazy eye). A talented storyteller, Eagle created the original storyline and playful characters for this book.

Mitchell Bagley is an orthoptist who has a keen interest in children with vision problems. He continues to collaborate with a large team of orthoptists and ophthalmologists to assist children of all ages, along with their families and carers, to overcome the difficulties of managing vision problems, including wearing glasses and eye patches, and administering eye drops. Mitchell is also involved in the university training of orthoptists, specifically in the diagnosis and therapeutic management of amblyopia and disorders of eye coordination.

Dr Jason Cheng is a Sydney-based ophthalmic surgeon who is passionate about promoting eye health. He has given public talks to local communities, promoted World Glaucoma Week on national media, and lectured at universities and international conferences. He has also volunteered in developing nations in Asia, Africa and the Pacific Islands, focusing on the education and training of local practitioners.

CPSIA information can be obtained
at www.ICGtesting.com
Printed in the USA
JSHW010140310121
11291JS00002B/5